Is Kentucky in the Sky?

Grandpa's Trip to Oklahoma Puzzles a Young Child

By Linda M. Penn

Illustrations by Donna Hardy
Colorations by Jara Coe

RACING TO JOY PRESS

Linda M. Penn
4-23-13

To Ally, Samantha, and Hunter

© Copyright 2012 by Linda M. Penn
Published by Racing to Joy Press, LLC

Illustrations by Donna Hardy and Colorations by Jara Coe
Peggy DeKay, Editor, Cover Design, Interior Layout
http://tbowt.com
peggy@tbowt.com

Summary

A young girl learns about distance and traveling when her Grandpa flies in an airplane from Kentucky to Oklahoma. In this book Allyson learns about airplanes, and abstract ideas like time and distance in a fun and entertaining way.

This is a concept book for early readers. All of Penn's books come complete with discussion questions in the appendix to help parents guide their children in getting the most from each book before, during, and after reading.

RACING TO JOY PRESS

"When can I go in an airplane?" Allyson asked. Allyson and her big sister Samantha help Mommy carry the bags of groceries into the kitchen.

"But you have been in an airplane," Samantha answered. "You don't remember because you were only a baby. We flew in an airplane to Kentucky, to see Grandpa."

"Grandpa has come in the airplane to see us the last two years—and he is coming to see us again. Today!"

"Grandpa is flying in a plane from Kentucky, where he lives, all the way to Oklahoma, where we live. It will be landing soon."

4

"Is Kentucky in the sky?" Allyson asked.

"No honey, now let's get these groceries put away," Mommy answered quickly. "Whoops!"

Mommy said as she tripped over the jar of peanut butter.

"Then, will you please check the bathroom to make sure the clean towels are out? Allyson, make sure your toys are picked up. Samantha, put your books away in your bookcase. Oh, don't forget to put away your clean clothes."

Allyson walked outside to the back yard and looked up into the sky. She was feeling puzzled. After a few minutes, Allyson came back inside to help Samantha put away the groceries.

"Allyson, we need to leave for the airport in ten minutes," Mommy said. They both grabbed for the sack with pretzels, cookies, and other yummy snacks.

They started ripping at the sack. Mommy looked at them with big eyes and shook her head.

"Okay," Samantha said, looking at Allyson. "You put away the bag of fun stuff. I'll take the heavy one with all the cans inside." Allyson and Samantha finished their jobs in the kitchen and bathroom, and then headed for their room.

Allyson walked over to her bedroom window. Instead of picking up her toys she looked up at the sky. "Is Kentucky in the sky? Is that why Grandpa is coming out of the sky to visit us?" she said to Samantha.

Samantha stopped hanging up her clothes and walked over to the window. "Kentucky is not up there in the sky," Samantha said as she rolled her eyes.

"Grandpa drives to the airport in Kentucky, gets on a plane, and then the pilot flies the plane to Oklahoma—through the sky."

Samantha began stacking her books in the bookcase. Allyson put away her toys. She noticed the Bible that Samantha had put in the bookcase.

Allyson remembered the Bible story about how God had made the world—the sky, land, water, sun, moon, and the stars. Her Sunday school teacher, Mr. Gilbert, told her this was called the Earth.

"Hey, Samantha, I got it now! Kentucky is land on God's earth just like Oklahoma is land on God's earth. Right?"

"Yes!" Samantha answered, giving Allyson a high-five. "Kentucky is far away from Oklahoma. Remember yesterday when we got in Mom's car and she drove to the city to visit her friend? That took about an hour."

"One hour? That was a long time. I got tired of sitting in the car seat," Allyson sighed.

"But Allyson," Samantha said, "if you stayed in your seat and Mom drove us on the land to Kentucky from Oklahoma, it would take ten hours."

Allyson started counting: "One, two, three, four, five, six, seven, eight, nine, ten. Wow! Ten hours is a really long time sitting."

Samantha was laughing as Mommy walked down the hall. Mommy was smiling too as she gave both of the girls a hug.

"Allyson, sorry that I didn't take the time to answer your question earlier," Mommy said. "It looks like you found the answer on your own."

"Yes Mommy. But I feel sorry for Grandpa—sitting for ten hours in a plane," Allyson said.

"It only takes two hours in a plane," Mommy said.

Allyson counted again. "One, two. That's only the next number after one. That's a lot different from counting all the way to ten."

"Mommy, I wouldn't get so tired of sitting if we go in a plane to visit Grandpa. Please, can we go?"

Mommy grinned as she said, "Next summer." Allyson ran down the hallway to the back door. "Come on Mommy! Come on, Samantha! Let's get to the airport. I can't wait to tell Grandpa about God's Earth!"

Discussion Questions

Before the Reading

From looking at the cover and reading the title, what do you think will be in this story?

From looking at the illustrations, have you changed your predictions? Why?

When do you last remember seeing an airplane in the sky?

Who might have been in that airplane?

Where could the airplane have come from and where could it have been going?

During the Reading

Why is Allyson so puzzled?

How are Allyson, Samantha, and Mommy preparing for Grandpa's visit?

Do you think Allyson and Samantha get along well? Why do you think this?

How does Samantha help Allyson solve the puzzle?

What Bible story does Allyson recall? Does this story help Allyson to solve the puzzle?

How?

Why does Mommy say she is sorry to Allyson?

What is Allyson going to tell Grandpa when she sees him?

After the Reading

Compare your predictions to what really happened in the story.

What would you tell a friend about this story?

Does the story remind you about anything that you and your family have done?

How?

Extra Fun with this Book

Many pages have a hidden kitty cat. Help your child find the hidden cat on those pages for additional activity and fun.

About the Author

 **Linda M. Penn** holds a Master's Degree and Rank I Degree in Elementary Education from the University of Louisville. She taught Kindergarten through third grade for 21 years in public schools. *Is Kentucky in the Sky* was the first book written by Penn and published by Racing to Joy Press, LLC.

During her teaching career and as a mother, she learned what kinds of books children loved to read. Her goal is to write books that children will read over and over again—books that stir their imagination.

Penn's other books, *Hunter and the FastCar Trophy Race* and *Clayton Makes New Friends* (available from Racing to Joy Press in 2012), are written to inspire young boys as they grow from emerging readers to fluent readers. Linda is now using her own life experiences with kids and her faith in God to write children's books. Penn's characters are modern and humorous, facing and solving real life kid problems.

Linda's website and blog, www.lindampenn.com has many resources for parents and children to enhance the reading experience. You can read her blog about writing for children and signup for additional educational resources for this book at her website.

Linda is available for school presentations, speaking opportunities, and conferences focusing on writing for children. Penn does presentations for public and private schools and home school organizations.

Contact the author at www.lindampenn.com or email her at lindampenn@gmail.com.

Illustrator and Colorist

 **Donna Hardy**, the illustrator, is a retired elementary and special education teacher. She graduated from Illinois State University with a Bachelor of Science in education and a Masters of Arts from the University of Evansville. She has taught elementary and middle school special education, kindergarten, second grade, and Title Math. She and her husband have two children and four grandchildren. Donna enjoys painting, traveling, backpacking, and horseback riding. She has co-authored *Jack Meets the New Baby* with Jara Coe and they are currently working on their second book.

 **Jara Coe**, the colorist, is a retired teacher with a Master's degree in Special Education and a minor in Library Science. She and her husband live in Indiana. They have two married children and five grandchildren. Her hobbies include painting and reading. *Jack Meets the New Baby* was her first children's book co-authored and illustrated with Donna Hardy.

Acknowledgements

Thanks to God for bringing this project together on His time schedule. I believe He brought Peggy DeKay, my teacher and book coach, into my life to make this project a reality. Thanks, Peggy.

Thanks to Ally, my granddaughter, for the idea for this story and for her encouragement. She actually asked the question, "*Is Kentucky in the Sky?*" as a three year old.

Thanks to Samantha and Hunter, the other grandkids, as they kept asking me, "Grandma, when are you getting the stories made into books?"

Thanks to Jeff, Vicki, and Pam for their critiques.

Thanks to Donna and Jara, the illustrators, who brought the characters to life.

Thanks to the Apple Store employees, who patiently assisted me with technical issues.

Thanks to Jason who keeps me working by maintaining my computer.

Thanks to Gil, Natalie, Jeff, Lisa, and David for your support.

Linda M. Penn

An Early
Concept Book

Early Concept Book

These books deal with abstract ideas for the young reader. All Early Concept Books help early readers to grasp abstract ideas. Early concept books come with questions at the end of the book. The discussions that come from asking these questions can enhance the learning experience for your child.

Beginning Reader

Beginning Reader books are for the beginning reader ages 4-6. These books also come with questions at the back of the book that may be used to enhance your child's learning experience.

Early Reader

Early Reader books are written for children who are learning to read on their own, ages 7-9. Questions in the back of the book may be used to enhance the learning experience for your child.

Young Reader

Young Reader books are designed for children reading on their own. These books are targeted to children ages 9-12.

Made in the USA
Charleston, SC
30 July 2012